RUPERT

and the
YELLOW
ELEPHANT

CARNIVAL

Rupert is up early this morning. It's his first day back at school after the summer holidays. He wishes the holidays were just beginning, not ending!

He yawns sleepily as Mrs Bear
pours his cornflakes. Something
else comes out with them – a free
gift!

Rupert picks it out of his bowl. It is a little model kit in bright yellow plastic.

He pours some milk on his cornflakes and reads the back of the packet. FREE ELEPHANT INSIDE! it says.

Rupert blinks. A free elephant –
in YELLOW! 'I don't think much
of that,' he mutters.

He breaks the pieces out of their
little frame and presses them
together. 'Thanks, Rupert,' says
a small voice.

Rupert stares at the elephant.
'Did YOU say that?' he gasps.

'I'm very hungry,' says the
elephant. 'I've been in that packet
for ages. Do you think I can have
some of your breakfast?'

Rupert watches in amazement as the elephant scrambles up the side of his bowl and jumps in.

Then he guzzles trunkfuls of milk, and rolls on his back in the soggy cornflakes.

'Hey, that's my breakfast you're squashing,' protests Rupert, finding his voice at last.

But the elephant just gives a cheeky grin and blows bubbles in the bowl, showering Rupert!

'Get out of there this minute,' cries Rupert, wiping his face.

He tries to pick up the elephant on the end of his spoon but the little jumbo wriggles away, splashing milk everywhere.

'Ho, ho, ho,' he laughs. 'This is a fine game, Rupert.'

Rupert looks at him firmly. 'If you don't come out,' he threatens, 'I'll wash you down the sink!'

'Don't do that,' squeals the elephant, clambering over the side, 'I've something very important to tell you.'

He sits on the edge of the butter dish. 'How can you tell if there is an elephant in your refrigerator?'

Rupert takes a deep breath. 'I don't think –' he begins.

'It's simple,' shrieks the elephant, leaping into the dish. 'Look for footprints in the butter!'

'Get off there,' roars Rupert.

'And there's another thing,' cries the elephant, jumping down from the butter dish and making a beeline for the marmalade. 'Do you know why elephants like me are coloured yellow?'

'I'm beginning to wonder,' says Rupert grimly.

'So that we can eat marmalade without being seen,' chortles the elephant, dropping into the jar.

'Oh no,' groans Rupert, trying to fish him out with a spoon. 'Whatever am I going to do with you?'

'This will make you laugh,' says the elephant when Rupert gets him out of the jar. He rushes across to the milk jug, fills up his trunk, and then squirts a stream of milk in Rupert's eye!

'Can you guess what I'm pretending to be?' he asks. But Rupert is too busy mopping his face again to answer.

'A jumbo jet,' howls the elephant, shaking with mirth.

'I shall be late for school if you don't stop this,' cries Rupert. 'I'm beginning to wish I'd never taken you out of the packet.'

'Don't say that,' grins the elephant. 'I promise you'll get to school on time – you can ride there on my back.'

Now it's Rupert's turn to laugh. 'I don't think you're big enough for that,' he says.

'Just watch me,' shouts the elephant, taking a deep breath.

To Rupert's amazement he starts to grow . . . and grow . . . and grow! In no time at all he is as tall as Rupert – and getting bigger.

'Stop!' calls Rupert as the elephant starts bumping against the sides of the little kitchen. 'There isn't enough room in here.'

But the elephant doesn't hear. He carries on growing and growing, and Rupert feels the walls shaking around him! Then, from a long way off, Rupert hears a voice calling. It is Mrs Bear.

She is shaking his shoulder.
'Wake up, Rupert,' she says
gently. 'You dozed off over
breakfast.'

Rupert blinks round, looking for
the elephant. But it has all been a
dream! The model kit is lying
untouched on the table.

Rupert puts it back in the cornflakes packet. 'I don't think I want this after all,' he says.

Mrs Bear wonders why. But Rupert decides not to tell her about the trouble you can have with a yellow elephant at breakfast!

Carnival
An imprint of the Children's Division
of the Collins Publishing Group
8 Grafton Street, London W1X 3LA

First published by Dragon Books 1986
Published by Carnival 1988

Written by Len Collis
Illustrated by Jon Davis
Designed by Ralph Semmence
Copyright © The Nutwood Press Ltd 1986
Copyright © Title and character of Rupert Bear,
Express Newspapers plc 1986

ISBN 0 00 1944 62 2

Printed & bound in Great Britain by
PURNELL BOOK PRODUCTION LIMITED
A MEMBER OF BPCC plc